O9-AIE-337

This book belongs to:

Disney's Out & About With Pooh

A Grow and Learn Library

Published by Advance Publishers

Written by Ronald Kidd
Illustrated by Arkadia Illustration Ltd.
Designed by Vickey Bolling
Produced by Bumpy Slide Books

ISBN:1-885222-62-9
10 9 8 7 6 5 4 3 2 1

It had been a blustery night in the Hundred-Acre Wood. The wind had raced across the sky, pushing clouds ahead of it and making the branches shiver.

By morning the wind had gone, and a breeze was blowing. The breeze lifted leaves from the trees and sent them drifting toward the ground. But one leaf never made it that far. Instead it landed on a nose.

It was a twitchy sort of nose, with whiskers on the sides and two large teeth below it. The nose belonged to Rabbit.

"A-a-a-choo!" said Rabbit, and the leaf floated to the ground.

Scratching his nose, Rabbit gazed sadly at his yard. It was covered with leaves. To Rabbit, that meant just one thing: work.

Rabbit went to his closet and put on the warmest scarf he could find. Bracing himself, he went outside into the chilly breeze.

He took a rake from his shed, then sighed and started raking leaves. There were a lot of leaves, and it would take him a long time to rake them all into neat little piles.

In another part of the forest, Winnie the Pooh was smiling. There was no special reason to smile. It was just that his mouth felt better when it was turned up than when it was turned down.

Humming a happy hum, Pooh looked out his window into the yard. It was covered with leaves. To Pooh, that meant just one thing: fun.

Pooh hurried outside. Throwing his arms open wide, he grinned up at the sky. As he did, he noticed a leaf floating in the breeze.

Pooh wondered what it was like to be a leaf. He decided to follow it, hoping to find out.

MR SANDERS
RNIG ALSO
HUNNY
HUNNY
HUNNY
HUNNY
HUNNY

The leaf drifted through the trees and spun past the pond and across the stream. Pooh had to run a little to keep up, but he stayed right behind it.

The leaf blew over a fence and into a pile of leaves, so Pooh jumped into the pile, too. He was lying there, thinking how pleasant it was to be a leaf, when he noticed Rabbit standing nearby.

“Hello, Rabbit,” said Pooh. “I was just having some fun. Would you care to join me?”

Rabbit stared at him. “Fun?” he said. “There’s work to be done! Don’t you know what season it is? Fall!”

So Pooh got up and fell down in the leaves again.

"Not that kind of fall," said Rabbit. "I'm talking about the season after summer. Fall is the time of year when plants and animals get ready for winter."

“For instance,” Rabbit said, “this maple tree is getting ready for winter by dropping its leaves. Then I have to rake them up.”

“That’s fun, isn’t it?” said Pooh.

“It most certainly is not,” answered Rabbit. “Work — that’s what fall is all about. Stick with me, Pooh, and I’ll show you.”

Rabbit led Pooh to his coat closet and handed him a scratchy brown scarf. “Fall is cold,” said Rabbit, “so you have to bundle up.”

But Pooh had his eye on a different scarf. “If you don’t mind,” he said, “I like this one better. It’s soft and it has pretty pictures on it.”

“It does?” said Rabbit. “I never noticed that.”

They went out to the pumpkin patch, where the ground was covered with fat, round pumpkins.

Rabbit said, “Fall is harvest time. That’s when you pick the vegetables that have been growing all summer, like these pumpkins. Would you like to help?”

Pooh nodded eagerly, and the two friends went to work.

Pooh picked his first pumpkin and rolled it to one side of the patch. He liked the way it rolled, so he rolled it some more. Pooh rolled the pumpkin to the top of a little hill, then sat down to admire it.

When he looked up a moment later, Rabbit was standing there, frowning.

"Pooh, what are you doing?" asked Rabbit.

Pooh said, “I was just thinking that this pumpkin reminds me of something. It has a nice, round shape, and it makes me happy to look at it.”

Suddenly it came to him. “I know what it reminds me of,” said Pooh. “It’s my tummy!”

Rabbit looked at the pumpkin, and his frown changed to a grin. “Yes, it does. It looks exactly like your tummy!”

Pooh patted his tummy, then patted the pumpkin. The pumpkin started to roll . . . and roll . . . and roll.

"My pumpkin!" cried Rabbit, and he took off chasing it.

The pumpkin rolled down the hill, picking up speed as it went. Pooh watched, amazed. Who would have thought that a fat pumpkin could go faster than a skinny rabbit?

The pumpkin began to bounce, past the pumpkin patch and into Rabbit's front yard. It hit the front door with a loud SPLAT! and stopped.

When Pooh came walking up a moment later, Rabbit said, "I think we've picked enough pumpkins for today, Pooh. Would you mind if we tried something else?"

Just then a squirrel scampered across the yard and Pooh asked, "What do squirrels do in the fall?"

Rabbit said, "They get ready for winter by saving food to eat when it's cold outside."

As Pooh and Rabbit watched, one of the squirrels scooped up some acorns, stuffed them into her cheeks, and hurried up a tree to her nest.

"We need to store food for the winter, too," said Rabbit. "If you're ready to go back to work, let's pick some apples."

He took Pooh to his orchard and they began picking the ripe, red fruit.

As Pooh plucked apples from the trees, he stuffed them into his cheeks, the way he'd seen the squirrel do.

A short time later, he went to Rabbit and asked a question. It sounded something like, "Prldl myl rbbuh, buh dl yuw hoff uh lddl smkkrl uff smthg? Hrl mng."

Rabbit looked at Pooh for a moment, then began to laugh. He laughed and laughed, and then he laughed some more.

Pooh tried to laugh, too, but it was hard to do with apples in his cheeks.

Pooh took the apples out of his mouth. Then he asked his question again, which turned out to be, “Pardon me, Rabbit, but do you have a little smackerel of something? Honey, I mean.”

Rabbit did indeed. He brought out a honey pot for Pooh and a shiny red apple for himself. The two friends sat by the edge of the forest, eating their snack and enjoying the bright fall day.

When Pooh finished, he said, “I’m sorry, Rabbit, but I think I’d better go home now. Most of me would like to keep working, but my cheeks are tired and need a nap.”

He started down the path, then stopped and called back, “Thank you for teaching me about fall, Rabbit. I had fun.”

After Pooh had left, Rabbit picked up his rake and headed for the maple tree to do more work. On the way, he saw a leaf floating in the breeze. Rabbit wondered what it was like to be a leaf. He knew what his friend Pooh would do if he were here.

Rabbit dropped his rake and began chasing the leaf through the forest. "My goodness," thought Rabbit, "fall *is* fun!"